D0607042

For Uma, forever and always

Special thanks to Dave, Nami, and Ann,
and, of course,
the REAL Beatrix and Kitty!

atheneum

ATHENEUM BOOKS FOR YOUNG READERS
An imprint of Simon & Schuster Children's Publishing Division
1230 Avenue of the Americas, New York, New York 10020
Copyright © 2015 by Lita Judge
All rights reserved, including the right of reproduction in whole or in part in
any form.
ATHENEUM BOOKS FOR YOUNG READERS is a registered trademark of
Simon & Schuster, Inc.
Atheneum logo is a trademark of Simon & Schuster, Inc.
For information about special discounts for bulk purchases, please
contact Simon & Schuster Special Sales at 1-866-506-1949 or
business@simonandschuster.com.
The Simon & Schuster Speakers Bureau can bring authors to your
live event. For more information or to book an event, contact the
Simon & Schuster Speakers Bureau at 1-866-248-3049 or visit
our website at www.simonspeakers.com.
Book design by Ann Bobco
The text for this book is set in Requiem, Eraser Dust, and Carrotflower.
The illustrations for this book are rendered in watercolor and pencil.
Manufactured in China
0215 SCP
First Edition
10 9 8 7 6 5 4 3 2 1
Library of Congress Cataloging-in-Publication Data
Judge, Lita, author, illustrator.
Good morning to me! / Lita Judge. — First edition.
pages cm
Summary: "A picture book about a parrot named Beatrix, who is very awake,
very excited to see her friends, and has a very hard time using her 'indoor
voice'"—Provided by publisher.
ISBN 978-1-4814-0369-6 (hardcover)
ISBN 978-1-4814-0370-2 (eBook)
[1. Parrots—Fiction. 2. Animals—Fiction. 3. Voice—Fiction. 4. Behavior—
Fiction. 5. Morning—Fiction.] I. Title.
PZ7.J894Go 2015
[E]—dc23   2014006270

GOOD MORNING TO ME!

by
LITA JUDGE

atheneum

Atheneum Books for Young Readers   New York - London - Toronto - Sydney - New Delhi

Early one morning in a little cottage,
Beatrix was wide AWAKE.
She knew it was time to be quiet,
but then she squealed,

"Good morning to me!"

"Look, there's Mouse.
Mouse is asleep.
I LOVE Mouse."

Beatrix tried to talk softly.

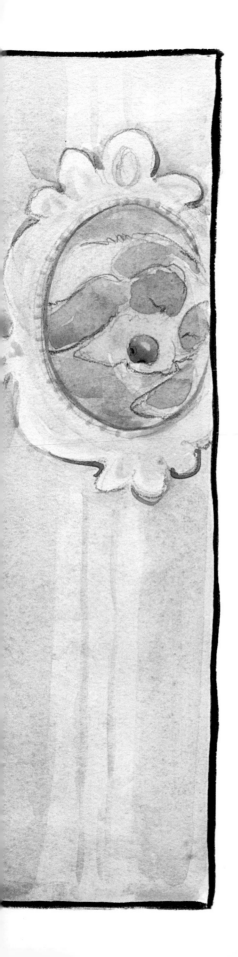

"I KNOW, I know—
indoor voice.
Today I'LL be a good birdie.
I promise, Mouse."

Beatrix climbed down from her perch.

"Watch me, Mouse."

"DAH...dut, DAH...dut, DAH...dut."

"Good, Gracie!" squealed Beatrix.
"Now put Birdie . . . down."

"What should we play next?"

!@*!!⨯!

Mouse was NOT AMUSED!

"I'm sorry, Mouse.

I promise, I'LL be a good birdie."

At last Beatrix was quiet.

Shhh . . . , she thought,
Mouse is asleep.

Then she
whispered . . .